Arthur and the
Popularity Test

A Marc Brown ARTHUR Chapter Book

Arthur and the Popularity Test

Text by Stephen Krensky
Based on the teleplay by Sandra Willard

Little, Brown and Company
Boston   New York   Toronto   London

First Edition

The characters and events portrayed in this book are fictitious. Any
similarity to real persons, living or dead, is coincidental and not intended
by the author.

Arthur® is a registered trademark of Marc Brown.

Text has been reviewed and assigned a reading level by Laurel S. Ernst,
M.A., Teachers College, Columbia University, New York, New York;
reading specialist, Chappaqua, New York

ISBN 0-316-11544-4 (hc)
ISBN 0-316-11545-2 (pb)
Library of Congress Catalog Card Number 98-66679

10 9 8 7 6 5 4 3 2 1

WOR (hc)
COM-MO (pb)

Published simultaneously in Canada by Little, Brown & Company
(Canada) Limited

Printed in the United States of America

For my dad, Bud

Chapter 1

• • • • • • • • • •

All across Elwood City, kids were getting ready to go to the community center.

"Be careful with those things," Sue Ellen's mother cautioned. "They're fragile."

"I'm always careful," said Sue Ellen. She wrapped up a gong of pounded metal, a gourd-shaped rattle, a small drum, and a tiny stringed instrument made of bent wood. Then she put them in her backpack.

"There," she said. "Perfect."

Over at Fern's house, Fern was filling her pack, too—with a cowbell and some rawhide strips.

"I think that's everything," she said. Then she looked up at her bookshelf. She pulled down a book.

But maybe I should just leave it home, she thought. I doubt anybody will be interested.

She started to put the book back.

Don't be such a coward, a voice in her head scolded. *Besides, even if you bring it, you can still chicken out at the last minute.*

"True enough," Fern sighed. She added the book to her pack and hurried out the door.

Francine was supposed to be going out her own door, too, but she wasn't ready yet.

"Oomph!" she grumbled, trying to fit a metal rod into her backpack. "This backpack just isn't big enough." It already held a whole bunch of wooden dowels and some bells.

"There's no way to make everything fit," she muttered.

Glancing around the room, she noticed her sister's backpack lying on her bed.

"Catherine," she said aloud, "your backpack is bigger than mine. Would you mind if I borrowed it today?"

"Of course not," she imagined Catherine replying. "After all, you're the best little sister in the whole world. So kind, so considerate. I can't refuse you anything. Take my clothes, my allowance . . ."

"Thank you," said Francine, smiling. "Just the backpack for now."

She emptied out her own pack and shoved all the contents into Catherine's.

At the Read house, Arthur had also given up on fitting everything in his backpack. He needed a large shopping bag, too. His father had put in a gourd, a bag of dried peas, some large tin cans, and a piece of

cheesecloth. He tied the bag tightly onto the back of Arthur's bike.

D.W. was watching. "Don't forget the kitchen sink," she told Arthur. "You've got everything else."

"Very funny," said Arthur.

Mr. Read finished fastening the bundle and stood up. "You certainly do have a lot here. These spring break activity days are pretty serious."

Arthur nodded. "Especially with Mr. Ratburn in charge."

His father gave the shopping bag one last pat. "You're really going to make musical instruments out of all this?" he asked.

"Sue Ellen has done it before," Arthur explained. "She says our group will have the best project in the whole community center."

"I look forward to seeing the results," said Mr. Read. "Maybe you can give a concert afterward."

"Maybe," said Arthur.

"If I made noise with those things," said D.W., "I'd get in trouble."

Arthur just smiled. "You might make noise," he said. "We're making music."

Chapter 2

• • • • • • • • • • •

As Arthur arrived at the community center, the stuff in the shopping bag rattled and clanked on his bike.

Buster and the Brain walked over to see what all the noise was about.

"What's that racket?" asked Buster.

Arthur laughed. "All the stuff I've brought to make musical instruments."

"It doesn't sound very musical," Buster noted.

"Whose idea was that project?" asked the Brain.

"Sue Ellen's," said Arthur. "She's in my group, along with Francine and Fern."

"You're lucky," said Buster. "We were assigned to Muffy and Jenna. It's hard getting them to agree to anything."

"Buster and I want to make some futuristic armor," said the Brain. "Muffy and Jenna want to weave baskets."

He and Buster both stuck out their tongues and made choking noises.

"Maybe you can figure out a way to combine your interests," said Arthur.

"Hmm, I'll put some thought into that," said the Brain.

"Wishful thinking," said Buster with a sigh.

When Arthur entered the crafts room, he took a seat at the table with Sue Ellen, Fern, and Francine.

"Did you bring everything?" Sue Ellen asked.

Arthur nodded. "My dad really loaded me up."

"Wait till you see what I've made

already," said Sue Ellen. She took out her instruments. "I made these at home. It's easy."

Arthur picked up the gourd rattle in one hand and tapped the drum with the other. "Hey," he said, "I can play both at the same time."

Fern cleared her throat. "I had an idea," she said hesitantly.

Everyone looked at her.

"Well, it's not a big idea, really. It's just something we could do along with the instruments."

She slid a book slowly out of her pack. Francine grabbed it.

"Poems," said Francine, frowning. "You've brought us poems?"

Fern nodded shyly. "I was thinking that we could read a poem while we play the instruments. Or I could read while you play. It would be a kind of performance."

"I don't think I'll be making poem music," said Arthur, rattling the gourd.

Francine put the book on the table. "And no one would hear the poem over the instruments, anyway."

Fern looked down. She was sorry she had even mentioned it. "Okay," she said quietly. "I guess you're right."

She slid the book away again.

Arthur dumped out all the stuff from his pack.

"Okay, here's everything from my dad." He looked at the pile. "I have one idea already."

He poured the dried peas into a can and covered it with cheesecloth. When he shook it, the can sounded like the gourd.

"Great!" said Sue Ellen.

"Let's see what we can do with my stuff," said Francine. She emptied out her pack. Along with her dowels, metal bar, and bells, there was a magazine.

"Hey!" said Francine. "This isn't mine. Oh, I get it. This must have been in Catherine's backpack already."

Arthur picked it up and looked at the cover.

"*Popular Girl*," he read aloud. He held it out at arm's length, as though it was radioactive. "Yuck! This is for teenage girls." He dropped it on the table. "I hope I didn't catch anything."

Francine, Sue Ellen, and Fern quickly huddled around the fallen magazine.

"Oooooh!" said Sue Ellen and Fern.

"Let me see," said Francine. "Remember, it came out of my pack."

"I hear that teen magazines have all sorts of strange and mysterious articles," said Sue Ellen.

"Do we dare look?" asked Fern.

"Of course," said Francine.

"But not now," said Mr. Ratburn, appearing from nowhere and sweeping up the magazine. He was in charge of the projects, and he planned to keep the kids focused.

"You can have this back at break time," he said.

The girls groaned, but there was nothing they could do. *Popular Girl* was just going to have to wait.

Chapter 3

· · · · · · · · · · ·

At break time, Francine, Sue Ellen, and Fern quickly ran outside to read *Popular Girl* at a picnic table. Arthur kept his distance from them, but he stayed close enough to hear everything they said.

"It says here you can get a prom date in twelve days or less," said Fern. "What's a prom?"

"Some kind of dance, I think," said Sue Ellen.

"And you have to wear a really uncomfortable dress," said Francine.

"How do you know that?" asked Fern.

"I heard Catherine talking about them.

Lots of times the dress won't even fit in a regular car. You have to take a limousine."

"That could be fun," said Sue Ellen.

Francine shuddered. "Not if you're uncomfortable. I'll bet you anything that those dresses itch, too."

Fern and Sue Ellen nodded.

"Did I hear someone mention dresses?" asked Muffy, who had just come outside with Jenna.

"*Uncomfortable* dresses," said Francine.

Muffy wasn't listening. "Is that *Popular Girl*?" she gasped.

The other girls nodded.

"I can't wait till I'm old enough to know what they're talking about," said Muffy. "Then I can do everything they say."

She pointed to a picture of a girl in a shiny green-and-orange-striped minidress. "I'll be just like that model." She sighed. "It'll be heaven."

Buster and the Brain came up behind her. They looked at the picture, too.

"That dress looks like one big lollipop," said Buster.

"An all-day sucker," the Brain added.

Muffy rolled her eyes. "As if you two know anything about fashion."

Francine flipped through a few more pages. "Here's a quiz," she said. " 'How likable are you?' "

"Let's take it," said Muffy. "I heard these tests can tell you a lot about yourself. Here, everyone take a piece of paper to write down your answers." She tore sheets from her notebook and handed them around.

Arthur, Buster, and the Brain laughed as they took their sheets.

"We don't need some dopey test to tell us if people like us," said Arthur.

"That's true," said Buster. "We can tell by the looks on their faces."

"Well, looks can be deceiving," Muffy reminded them.

"Never mind the boys," said Fern, who had found some pencils in her pack and was passing them out. "What does it say?"

Francine read on. " 'Question number one: If you were a sandwich, would your friends be (a) potato chips, (b) diet soda, (c) the plate, or (d) hungry?' "

"Definitely potato chips," said Arthur.

"I agree," said the Brain.

"This test is making me hungry," said Buster. "Did anybody bring a snack?"

The girls all ignored them and wrote down their answers.

Francine read the next question. " 'If you could bring one thing to a desert island, would it be (a) your telephone, (b) your mirror, (c) your ten-speed blow-dryer, or (d) your kitchen?' "

"This one's harder," said Fern.

Francine bit her tongue in thought before making her choice.

But before she could continue, a huge gust of wind blew the magazine off the table. It spun end over end — and landed in a mud puddle.

"Is it still readable?" Fern asked anxiously.

Francine ran over and picked up the soggy, dripping bundle of glop. "Sorry," she said. "I don't think this patient is going to make it." She dropped the magazine into the trash can.

"Oh, well," said Sue Ellen. "That's the end of that."

Chapter 4
• • • • • • • • • • •

When Francine and Arthur got on their bikes at the end of the day, they were still talking about the test.

"It was weird," said Arthur. "Those questions were so strange! And even stranger answers. Who would think of a friend as a potato chip?"

"The test was written for teenagers," Francine explained. "So you never know what to expect. Teenagers don't think the way we do."

"They don't?" Arthur stopped to consider this. "That's what I'm always thinking about D.W., too. Hey, you don't suppose she's a teenager in disguise?"

Francine laughed. "No, I think we're just surrounded by craziness. Believe me, I've watched my sister Catherine in action."

"Scary?" Arthur asked.

"Very. Sometimes, when I'm lying in bed, I think about Catherine and her friends and try to imagine being their age — the way they talk and dress . . ." Francine shuddered. "After that, I can't sleep for hours."

"Thanks for cheering me up, Francine."

"Life is hard, Arthur. You'd better get used to it."

"Oh, really? And I suppose you're an expert. . . ."

They continued the conversation as they rode off down the street.

Fern watched them go. As soon as they

rounded the corner, she ran over to the trash can. Then she pulled out Francine's magazine. *Popular Girl* did not look very crisp, but at least it had dried out.

Fern sat down on the steps, trying to separate the pages.

"What are you doing?" asked Sue Ellen.

Fern jumped. "Oh, it's you. I thought everyone had left."

"I was talking to Mr. Ratburn for a minute. He had a question about how to tune some of the instruments. He was . . . Are you listening to me?"

"Sorry," Fern said. "I was just concentrating on trying to read this through the wrinkles."

Sue Ellen frowned. "Why bother?" she asked.

"I just wanted to answer the rest of the questions. At the end you can find out how likable you are. It says it's very scientific."

"So?"

Fern smoothed out the pages. "Aren't you curious about yourself?"

"No." Sue Ellen paused. "Well, maybe a little." She sat down on the steps next to Fern. "So what do we have to do?"

"Finish the test."

"Okay," said Sue Ellen. "So where were we?"

They went through the rest of the questions, including one asking about their superstitions, another on what they would say when meeting aliens from other planets, and the last, which asked what kind of movie was best for a first date.

"How are we supposed to know all this stuff?" said Sue Ellen.

"The directions say there are no wrong answers," said Fern. "Just choose what feels right."

Some minutes later, both girls were done.

"I think my feelings are all used up," said Sue Ellen.

"Mine, too," said Fern. "Now we should figure out our scores. Then we'll know what to do next."

Chapter 5

• • • • • • • • • • •

Fern turned to the answer page.

"Are you nervous?" asked Sue Ellen.

"A little," Fern admitted. "Of course, that doesn't prove much. I'm nervous a lot."

"Just remember, it's only one test."

Fern nodded. "I always say that when I don't expect to do very well." She totaled her points and checked the answer key.

"I got a twelve," she said finally.

"Is that good?" asked Sue Ellen.

"Let's see what it says. Hmmm . . . 'If you score less than twenty, you are too quiet. You might be likable, but nobody would know it because nobody knows you're there.' "

Fern looked at Sue Ellen in horror. "Oh, no, that's my worst nightmare!"

Everyone was at their seats as Mr. Ratburn took attendance.

"Buster . . . Muffy . . . Where is Fern? She's been absent for four days."

"Here I am!" cried Fern from the back of the class. But nobody looked up when she spoke.

"I don't understand it," Fern muttered. Then she looked down at herself—and gasped.

She was transparent!

"I'm like a sheet of glass," said Fern. "I can see right through me—and that must mean everyone else can, too."

"Tsk, tsk," said Mr. Ratburn. "I don't know what Fern is thinking. I'm going to have to call her parents."

"Oooooh!" the class said together.

"But I'm right here!" Fern shouted. It didn't help. No one could hear her.

The bell rang, and the kids filed out for recess. They all walked right through Fern.

"This is terrible," she sighed.

"Is there any hope?" asked Sue Ellen.

Fern blinked. "I don't know." She looked farther down the page. "Yes, yes, they have advice. 'Be strong,' it says. 'A low score means you hesitate to speak your mind. Say what you want, whether anyone wants to hear it or not.' "

"Now it's my turn," said Sue Ellen. She looked over the answer key for herself. "I scored 125."

"That's great!" said Fern. "Isn't it?"

Sue Ellen shook her head. "It says here that 'if you scored over 120, then you are too good to be true. You frighten people with your excellence. Tone it down!' "

Sue Ellen lowered the magazine. She was shocked.

"Well," said Fern, "you *are* good at everything, Sue Ellen."

Sue Ellen stopped to think about it.

In the band room at school, Sue Ellen, Binky, Francine, Buster, and Arthur were practicing. Sue Ellen was playing a sax solo.

Suddenly Buster stood up and dropped his tuba in despair.

"Oh, what's the point?" he said. "I'll never be as good as you, Sue Ellen."

Arthur banged his head on the keyboard. "I'm frightened by her excellence."

Binky stared at her, then at his clarinet. "I might as well stick my tongue in a drawer and never blow again."

Everyone stormed out, leaving Sue Ellen blowing a last sour note.

"What am I going to do?" said Sue Ellen.

"What are *we* going to do?" Fern corrected her.

Sue Ellen was silent. Then she snapped her fingers. "Wait a minute. We have friends. So this test must be wrong. Right?" She looked hopefully at Fern.

"Well, this magazine is for teenagers," Fern reminded her. "So it must be predicting the future. Our future!"

Sue Ellen covered her mouth with her hands.

"It's not too late," said Fern. "This test is a warning."

Sue Ellen lowered her hands.

"Starting tomorrow," Fern said firmly, "we have to change." She took a deep breath. "If we don't, we'll become friendless for the rest of our lives."

Chapter 6

•••••••••••

The next day, all the kids were sitting on gym mats in front of Mr. Ratburn. He was wearing a karate *gi* and bowed to them before speaking.

"This morning," he said, "we will focus on karate. Let's have a demonstration from our expert, Sue Ellen."

Sue Ellen was standing next to Fern. "Who? Me?" she said. "I'm not an expert, Mr. Ratburn. I'm just average. Barely."

Mr. Ratburn nodded. "Yes, yes, we appreciate your modesty, Sue Ellen. Now, step up here onto the mat. Good. All right, I need another volunteer. Who shall it be? Ah, thank you, Buster. Step on up."

Buster looked down at his hands. "Me?" he squeaked. "Against Sue Ellen? Well . . . okay. . . ."

"Begin," said Mr. Ratburn.

The two opponents stared at each other. Buster waited for Sue Ellen to make one of her lightning moves and throw him on his back. But Sue Ellen didn't move. Finally Buster darted in and took Sue Ellen's arm. When she offered no resistance, he dipped his hip—and flipped her over.

The other kids gasped.

"Excellent," said Mr. Ratburn.

Buster was shocked. "I flipped Sue Ellen? Wow! I must be good."

Fern leaned down to Sue Ellen on the mat. "See?" she whispered. "It's working."

Sue Ellen just made a face.

Binky stepped onto the mat. "If Buster can do that, so can I."

"Hold on," said Mr. Ratburn. "Sue Ellen, do you want another match?"

She nodded weakly. "I guess so."

"Very well."

A moment later, Binky rushed in, and once again Sue Ellen didn't resist. She was soon lying on her back again, facing the ceiling.

Binky raised his arms victoriously, but only for a moment. Then he dropped them abruptly.

"This victory stinks," he said, helping to pull Sue Ellen to her feet.

She looked surprised. "Why? Doesn't it make you feel good about yourself?"

Binky looked at her suspiciously. "Why would I want to . . . Hey! You did that on purpose, didn't you? You weren't even trying."

Sue Ellen looked away.

"Well, *I'm* trying," Fern said suddenly. She stepped onto the mat. For a second she seemed ready to face Binky. Then she changed her mind and turned to Buster instead.

"Try me," she said.

"Huh?" said Buster. "Okay." After beating Sue Ellen, he didn't expect any problems with Fern.

Fern waved her arms in a blur and released a yell. "Eeeyahhhhh!"

Buster stumbled back, losing his balance. Seeing her chance, Fern lunged forward, grabbed him, and tossed him down.

"Oomph!" said Buster.

Fern jumped up and down excitedly. "I did it! I did it!"

"All right, all right," said Mr. Ratburn. "I think that's enough demonstrating for today."

Arthur went over to Buster, who was still on his back, staring upward.

"You flipped Sue Ellen," he said. "And then Fern flipped *you*."

Buster nodded. "It feels like the world's turned upside down."

As the group turned to another activity, Fern and Sue Ellen could see the other kids watching them.

"It's working," Fern whispered. "Everyone's staring at us. That must mean we're likable."

"I hope you're right," said Sue Ellen, rubbing her shoulder. "I'm not sure how much more being liked I can take."

Chapter 7

• • • • • • • • • • •

The Brain, Jenna, Muffy, and Buster were weaving on a loom in the community center. Or trying to. There was a big knot in the thread, and Buster was untangling it.

"We need help," he said. "Oh, look, there's Sue Ellen. She'll know what to do."

Sue Ellen entered the room with Fern. "Help with what?"

"Our group is weaving a futuristic, non-cuttable armor fabric," said the Brain. "But we've run into some, ah, snags." . He glanced at Muffy. "I know you've done some weaving. Do you have any suggestions?"

"Well," Sue Ellen began, "I remember doing—" She stopped because Fern had elbowed her in the side.

"Go on," said the Brain.

"Actually I don't remember that much. I'm sure any ideas you have will be better than mine."

She turned and walked off. But Fern took a moment to look at their work.

"Silver?" she said. "Who made that choice?"

"We all did," said the young weavers.

"Puh-leeze," said Fern. "It will clash with everything. Trust me, go with red." Then she ran to catch up with Sue Ellen.

"Red?" said the Brain. "Where did that come from?"

No one knew.

A little later, Arthur and Francine were working hard on their instruments. Sue Ellen was sitting with them.

Francine bent a thin aluminum pipe into a lopsided triangle. Then she hit it with a metal rod.

Clunk.

Sue Ellen forced a smile.

Meanwhile, Arthur was stretching rubber bands on a wooden frame. He let go of one of them — and it ricocheted around the room, hitting Francine in the arm.

"Ow!" said Francine.

"Sorry," said Arthur.

"Sue Ellen," said Francine, "weren't you going to show us how to make idiotphones?"

"Not *idiotphones*," Sue Ellen explained. "Idiophones. An idiophone is any instrument that vibrates when it's struck and makes a noise, like a gong or a drum or —" She hesitated as Fern came in. "I mean, that's what I think it is. I'm probably wrong."

"Probably," Fern agreed, pulling the book of poems out of her backpack.

"Listen up, everyone," she said. "I've chosen the poem I'm going to read. Arthur, you and Francine will accompany me."

"We will?" said Arthur. "Wait. When did we decide that?"

"You didn't," said Fern. "I did. This group needs leadership, so I'm providing it."

"This group doesn't need a leader," said Francine. "Right, Sue Ellen?"

"Well, um—"

Fern folded her arms. "Sue Ellen and I have already discussed this. We've agreed that she has no opinion."

Francine stood up. "Maybe not," she said. "But I do. If you want to boss people around, find your own group."

She took her metal triangle and left.

"You two are sure acting very strange," said Arthur.

Then he followed Francine out the door.

Fern watched them go. "Do you think I was strong enough?" she asked Sue Ellen.

"Oh, yes," said Sue Ellen. "They definitely know you're here now. There's no missing you at this point."

"Good." Fern sighed. "At least I think it's good. Our plan is working out well, isn't it?"

Sue Ellen tried to smile because she didn't know what to say.

Chapter 8

• • • • • • • • • • •

Arthur and Francine were sitting by a wall, trying to play their instruments.

Arthur was having particular trouble getting his rubber bands to stay put.

Sprunngg!

"There goes another one," he said. "They're all either too tight or too loose. I was counting on Sue Ellen to help me with this part. But she keeps telling me to do it my own way." He scratched his head. "She was never shy with her opinions before."

"And Fern's become just the opposite,"

Francine muttered. "I liked the old Fern better. She was quiet, but I always felt like she listened to what I had to say. Now she's just a bossy know-it-all. Oooh! They both make me so mad."

She pounded on a gourd as she spoke, and her hand broke through the side.

"Hey!" said Francine. "I'm stuck."

She waved her hand around with the gourd on the end of it.

Across the room, the Brain and Jenna were hopelessly tangled up in the loom. Buster looked like a mummy in red and silver as he tried to untie the different knots.

Muffy folded her arms in disgust.

"This is ridiculous," she said. "It's all Sue Ellen's fault."

"I don't follow your logic," said the Brain. "She's not even part of our group."

"Sue Ellen knows how to weave,"

Muffy insisted. "She could have helped us. But, no, she stayed away. Wait till I give her a piece of my mind."

"Well, at least we're better off than Binky," said Buster. He pointed to the corner of the room, where Binky was lying on the floor, wearing a large papier-mâché horse's head.

Molly, Rattles, and Prunella were squatting around him, trying to apply some finishing touches of paint.

"Binky, you have to get up now!" said Prunella. "We can't reach the back with you lying on the floor."

"Why did she do it?" came the muffled voice from inside the horse's head.

Prunella shook her head. "Are you still talking about that?"

The horse's head nodded. "I've been trying to figure it out. But I just don't understand."

Molly groaned. "Sue Ellen wasn't making fun of you."

"She faked a fall," Binky went on. "It's so insulting. She doesn't even think I'm worth flipping anymore."

"We'll be flipping you in another minute," said Rattles, pulling Binky up to a sitting position. "Then we'll take on Sue Ellen and Fern!"

Mr. Ratburn surveyed the room in dismay. "What's happening?" he moaned. "I thought everything was going so well."

He scurried around, trying to calm everyone down and help out wherever he could.

Behind him, Sue Ellen and Fern looked on in disbelief. They had heard most of what everyone had said. Was it possible they had made such a big mistake? Where had they gone wrong?

And how could they make it right again?

Chapter 9

• • • • • • • • • • •

Fern and Sue Ellen snuck out of the building, clutching their copy of *Popular Girl*. The sun was shining, but they didn't notice. As far as they were concerned, dark clouds hung over their heads.

"Maybe there's another test in here we can take," said Fern. "A second test for when the first test doesn't work."

"I'm not sure it will be enough," said Sue Ellen. "We might need ten tests just to get things back to normal."

Fern flipped through the pages. "What if we missed something?"

Sue Ellen wasn't very hopeful. "I

wouldn't count on it. I think we followed the directions perfectly."

She sat down on the steps and cupped her chin in her hand.

"Things should have turned out differently," Fern insisted, sitting down beside her. "Our future was supposed to look like this."

She held up a muddy photo of a smiling teenage girl. The girl was surrounded by her equally smiling friends. They all looked incredibly happy. They also had very white teeth and no pimples.

"That's what I had in mind," said Fern. "The test made me afraid that if we didn't change, we would lose the friends we already have." She pointed at the picture. "Then we'd *never* be like her."

"You mean," said a voice behind them, "you've been acting this way because of that stupid popularity test?"

Fern and Sue Ellen turned. Francine,

Arthur, and Buster had come up behind them. Francine was still wearing the gourd on one hand.

"It's not stupid," said Fern. "It's scientific. It says so right in the introduction."

"And we carefully answered each question," said Sue Ellen. "Some of them were really tough."

"Did you answer that your friends were diet soda?" Buster asked. "That might have thrown off your score."

Fern sighed. "I don't think diet soda played any part in it, Buster. The test results said that Sue Ellen draws too much attention to herself, while I, um, don't draw any attention at all. And that we aren't likable because of that."

"But that's not true," said Arthur. "We like you the way you are."

"But the test was so definite . . . ," said Fern.

"Maybe," said Francine, "but that test

was designed for teenagers, remember? The results wouldn't match up for us, because we're younger and smarter than they are."

Fern hadn't considered that. "So you don't think I'm too quiet?" she asked.

"And that I'm too good to be true?" Sue Ellen added.

"No!" Francine, Arthur, and Buster said together.

Fern and Sue Ellen smiled in relief.

"Now, if we have that settled," said Arthur, "will you please come in? We still need help with our instruments."

"If you insist," said Sue Ellen.

"After you," Fern told her.

Then they both jumped up happily and followed the others inside.

Chapter 10

• • • • • • • • • • • •

Mr. Ratburn stood at the door to the community center, talking to the kids as they left.

"This has been a fun week!" he exclaimed. "Great projects, everyone! We'll see you back in school on Monday."

Muffy came out with a square of silver fabric. Buster, Jenna, and the Brain followed her.

"How can we split this up?" Muffy asked. "It won't cut."

"Maybe we could share," said Buster.

The Brain laughed. "That's what we get for creating non-cuttable fabric."

"Whose bright idea was that, anyway?" asked Jenna.

The Brain and Buster pointed at each other.

"Look out! Look out for ancient Greece's mightiest secret weapon, the Trojan horse!"

Prunella came out, pushing the completed Trojan horse. Molly and Rattles were helping her. Underneath the horse, two feet were sticking out.

"Who's in there?" asked Buster.

Suddenly the side opened — and Binky stuck his head out.

"Greeks rule and Trojans drool!"

The sound of music followed this comment as Arthur, Francine, Sue Ellen, and Fern came out, playing their homemade instruments.

Arthur plucked his rubber bands while Francine shook her repaired gourd.

"Wait till D.W. hears this," said Arthur.

"She'll go crazy." He smiled at the thought.

Francine nodded. "I can't wait to give Catherine a performance."

Sue Ellen ran forward to catch up to Binky.

"I wanted to talk to you," she said.

Binky frowned. "What do *you* want?" he asked.

"I thought I'd offer you a rematch," said Sue Ellen.

Binky thought it over. "And you'll do your best?" he asked.

Sue Ellen laughed. "You can depend on it."

"Good," said Binky. Then he noticed the determined look on Sue Ellen's face. "At least I think it's good."

"I'm glad to see all's well that ends well," said Mr. Ratburn. "And I'll bet everyone was happy to have a whole week without having to take a single test."

Sue Ellen and Fern just looked at each other.

"We wish!" they said together.